The Twelve Days of Christmas

Bob Chilcott

for SATB, piano, and percussion

Vocal score

MUSIC DEPARTMENT

OXFORD
UNIVERSITY PRESS

OXFORD
UNIVERSITY PRESS

Great Clarendon Street, Oxford OX2 6DP, England
198 Madison Avenue, New York, NY10016, USA

Oxford University Press is a department of the University of Oxford.
It furthers the University's aim of excellence in research, scholarship,
and education by publishing worldwide in

Oxford New York
Auckland Bangkok Buenos Aires Cape Town Chennai
Dar es Salaam Delhi Hong Kong Istanbul Karachi Kolkata
Kuala Lumpur Madrid Melbourne Mexico City Mumbai Nairobi
São Paulo Shanghai Taipei Tokyo Toronto

5 7 9 10 8 6 4

ISBN 978-0-19343327-4

Music and text origination by
Jeanne Roberts
Printed in Great Britain on acid-free paper by
Halstan & Co. Ltd., Amersham, Bucks.

Composer's note

This piece was originally written for the Final of Sainsbury's Choir of the Year in 2000, and subsequently revised for the same event in 2002. The main idea behind it was to provide a small 'solo' for the soloists, ensembles, and choirs guesting at both events by turning the 'five gold rings' refrain into a tailor-made, miniature 'showcase' for each of them.

A distinguished list of performers took part. Two choirs, the Scunthorpe Co-operative Junior Choir and the London Adventist Chorale in conjunction with the Croydon Seventh Day Adventist Gospel Choir, were common to both performances. Singers appearing at one or other of the events included Ruby Turner, Jason Howard, the King's Singers, the Cambridge Chord Company, Cantores Novae, the Exmoor Singers, Sharon Clarke, the Opera Babes, the BBC Singers, Matrix, the Berkshire Youth Choir, and Choros Amici.

This version of the piece is for one SATB choir, but it retains the flexibility to include 'guest' ensembles or soloists. The audience can also join in with the 'chorus'. The most important thing is to have fun with it!

I am grateful to Terry Edwards for giving me the 'five gold rings' idea, and to Bill Kallaway for enabling it to happen.

Duration: *c.*10 minutes

In the original version of this piece, the percussion part was scored for two players, and the piano accompaniment for piano duet (or two pianos). These parts are compatible with the current version of the vocal score, and are available to purchase from the publisher:

Original percussion parts 1 and 2 (ISBN 978–0–19–343332–8)
Original piano duet/two pianos (ISBN 978–0–19–343331–1)

Additionally, the percussion part for single player as scored in the current version is available to purchase from the publisher:

Single percussion part (ISBN 978–0–19–343338–0)

A version of the accompaniment scored for full orchestra (piccolo, flute, two oboes, two clarinets, two bassoons, two horns, two trumpets, two trombones, bass trombone, timpani, two percussion players, harp, and strings) is available to hire from the publisher.

*Commissioned by Sainsbury's Choir of the Year 2000 for Choirs Galore
at the Royal Albert Hall, London, conducted by Terry Edwards.
Revised 2002 for Sainsbury's Choir of the Year 2002.*

The Twelve Days of Christmas

English traditional

adapted and arr. **BOB CHILCOTT**

OXFORD UNIVERSITY PRESS, MUSIC DEPARTMENT, GREAT CLARENDON STREET, OXFORD OX2 6DP

8

two___ tur - tle doves, and a par - tridge in a pear___ tree.

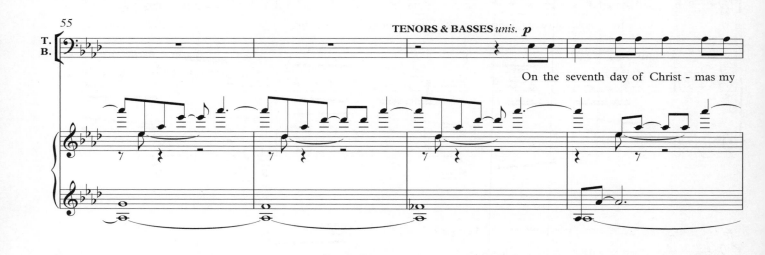

TENORS & BASSES *unis.* **p**

On the seventh day of Christ - mas my

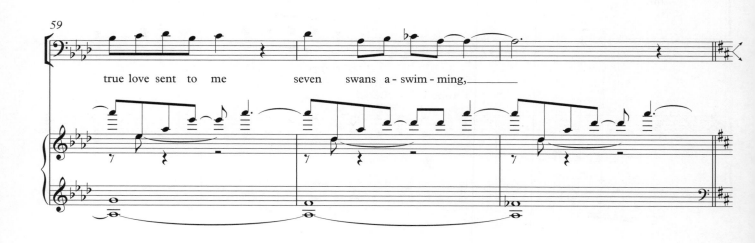

true love sent to me seven swans a - swim - ming,___

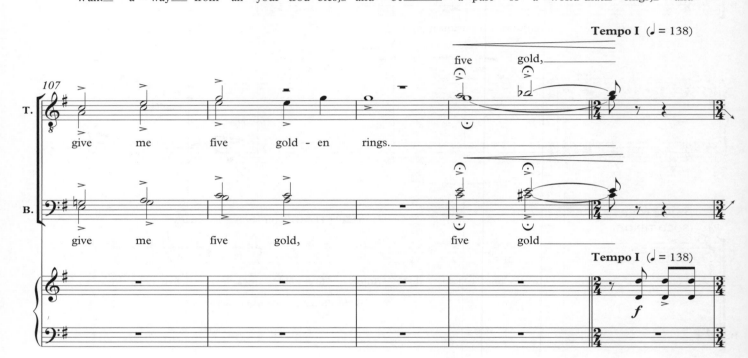

On the ninth day of Christ-mas my true love sent to me

la la la la la la la la la

nine la-dies dan-cing,

la eight maids a-milk-ing,

seven swans a-swim-ming,

Tambourine

tree.

Funky and hard ♩ = *c.*120

six geese a - lay - ing,

f (ad lib.)

p

Drum kit (ad lib.)

mf

f

Give me five, O give me five gold rings, give me five, O

f

give me five gold rings, give me five, O give me five gold rings._____

_____ Give me five, O give me five gold rings, give me five, O

245 Rock gospel style ♩. = 63

mf

Goin' to sing a song___ for my Je - sus, a

(ad lib.)
mf

Drum kit (ad lib.)
mf

248

song that gives me wings,___ drink the wa - ter___ from the foun - tain,___ from

cresc.

cresc.

cresc.

250

f

where His love___ springs. Goin' to praise my God, goin' to praise my God, with

f

f

praise my God,   goin' to praise my God   with   ev - 'ry voice that   sings___

five gold, five   gold_ rings._   Goin' to   praise my God, goin' to praise my God,   with

30

two___ tur - tle doves, and a par - tridge___ in a pear tree._____